FLY GUY VS. THE FLYSWATTER!

Tedd Arnold

CARTWHEEL BOOKS
An Imprint of Scholastic Inc.

For Brianna!

ISBN 978-0-545-65580-4

12 11 10 9 8 7 6   14 15 16 17 18 19/0

Printed in the U.S.A.   40

This edition first printing, January 2014

A boy had a pet fly.
He named him Fly Guy.
And Fly Guy could
say the boy's name—

BUZZ!

Chapter 1

One day, Fly Guy was eating breakfast in Buzz's backpack.

Buzz grabbed his backpack
and went to school.

At school, Fly Guy
flew out.

Then the teacher said,
"We are going on a field trip
to tour a factory."

Buzz said, "Fly Guy, you can ride in my pocket."

The class rode the bus to the factory.

They arrived at the factory.

Chapter 2

A tour guide led the
class inside.

Buzz said, "Fly Guy,
stay down in my pocket!"

The tour guide said, "Here is our flyswatter museum."

"Here is where we make the flyswatters," she said. "You may each have one."

"Now," said the guide, "here is Fred the Fly to tell you more!"

Fly Guy peeked out.

"Boys and girls," said Fred.
"We know flies play in slime."
Fly Guy nodded.

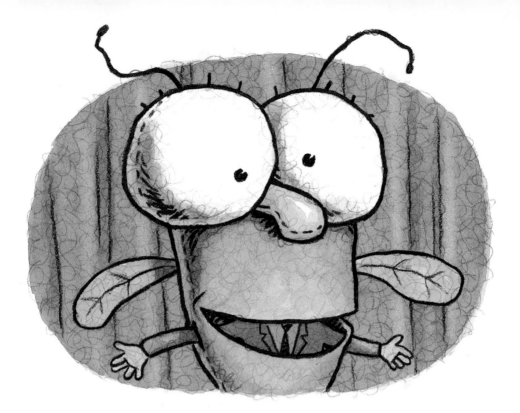

"Flies eat garbage!"
Fly Guy smiled.

"Flies are nasty!"
Fly Guy got mad.

"That's why, boys and girls,"
Fred the Fly shouted,
"we need . . .

the flyswatter of the future—
the **Super Swatter 6000!**"

Chapter 3

"Now let's see what the Super Swatter can do!" said Fred. "Bring out the fly!"

The tour guide brought
out a tiny fly in a jar.

"Release the fly!"
yelled Fred.

The Super Swatter
started swatting.

Fly Guy cried,

Fly Guy flew to the little fly.

The Super Swatter kept swatting.

Fly Guy took the fly
to an open window.

The Super Swatter kept swatting.

WHAP
WHAP
WHAP
WHAP
WHAP

Fly Guy flew past
Fred the Fly.

WHAP

WHAP

WHAP

WHAP

WHAP

WHAP

WHAP

WHAP

The Super Swatter kept swatting.

Fly Guy flew past the
flyswatter machines.
The Super Swatter kept swatting.

"Stop! Stop!" yelled Fred.
"Everyone out! No more
factory tours, ever!"

Back at school, the class
made an art project. Everyone
agreed—